Special thanks to OPTIMUS Health Care whose Behavioral Health team collaborated on the creation of this book. Helen Collins LCSW and Brianna Whitlock LCSW, were invaluable contributors providing expert insight to ensure the content was thoughtfully crafted for young readers experiencing school bus anxiety.

OPTIMUS Health Care is Southwest Connecticut's leading provider of comprehensive, community-based health services, committed to advancing wellness and supporting the emotional and physical health of children and families.

—

For more information on Optimus and their services please visit...
optimushealthcare.org

Lily stood by the window clutching her backpack and gazed nervously out the window looking for the big yellow bus. Today was the big day - her first time riding the bus to school. The thought made her stomach flutter like butterfly wings! Her cheeks felt warm and her hands were a little sweaty as she gripped her backpack straps tighter.

"Don't worry sweetheart," her mom said with a comforting smile as she crouched down beside her. "It's going to be fun, like an adventure! You'll see new things, meet new friends, and have stories to tell when you come home."

Her mom gently placed a hand on Lily's shoulder. "And remember, if you start feeling nervous on the bus, try looking out the window and notice all the interesting things that pass by. Sometimes when we focus on what's around us, those butterfly feelings calm down." The word "adventure" did sound exciting to Lily, but she was still a little nervous.

Lily and her mom went to the bus stop and heard the rumble of the engine as the big yellow bus came down the street, slowed down, and stopped right in front of them. The door opened with a soft "whoosh," and a smiling driver waved.

"Hello! I'm Mrs. Jones," said the bus driver warmly. "I'll make sure you have a safe and smooth ride and we will always wait for you to be safely seated before we start moving." Hearing Mrs. Jones' kind voice and seeing her friendly smile made Lily feel more welcome. She took a deep breath and felt ready to take that first step onto the bus.

Lily climbed aboard. The bus was warm and cozy inside, and the seats were just the right size. There were other kids on the bus, and Lily chose a seat by the window.

As the bus started to move, Lily felt the gentle rolling of the wheels. Remembering her mom's advice, she looked out the window and began to notice everything around her. She saw bright houses, tall trees, people walking their dogs, and a pond with ducks paddling. As she focused on all these details, her nervousness began to melt away just like her mom had said it would.

At the next stop, a new passenger stepped onto the bus. "Hi! I'm Milo, can I sit with you?" he asked with a friendly grin. Lily felt a little shy at first, but she remembered that making new friends was part of the adventure. She smiled back and said, "Yes! I'm Lily, and this is my first time on the bus." "That's so cool!" Milo said as he settled into the seat beside her. "I was nervous my first time too, but now I love it!"

As the bus started to move again, the two talked about their favorite animals and colors. Milo started pointing out fun sights like a big red tractor in a field and a house with a garden full of bright flowers. Having someone to talk to made the ride feel even more comfortable and fun.

By the time the bus reached school, Lily felt like an explorer who had discovered something amazing. "I think I really like riding this bus!" Lily said to Milo, who grinned in agreement.

Mrs. Jones told everyone to wait until the bus came to a complete stop before getting up from their seats, and to use the handrails when walking off. "Let's be safe together!" she announced cheerfully. Lily carefully followed the safety rules and stepped off the bus feeling proud and excited for her first day at school.

**At the end of the day, the ride home was even better. Lily and Milo saw more exciting sights...**

a cat napping on a porch

kids playing in a park

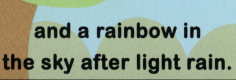
and a rainbow in the sky after light rain.

Lily and Milo laughed and shared stories about their school day. The ride home seemed to go by so fast as they were having such a good time together.

When the big yellow bus stopped at Lily's house, her mom was waiting with a big smile. Mrs. Jones waved goodbye and said, "See you tomorrow for our next big yellow adventure!"

From that day on, Lily loved riding the big yellow bus. Whether it was spotting fun sights through the window, making new friends, or listening to Mrs. Jones' cheerful voice, every ride was special. What started as a nervous morning became a fun adventure every day. And Lily learned something important: sometimes when you face something new, it turns out better than you could ever imagine!

# DATTCO

# SCHOOL BUS SAFETY TIPS

**EXIT** Never play with the emergency exits

Hold the handrail while going up and down the stairs

Never throw things on the bus or out the windows

Keep the aisles/floor clear at all times

# HOW LILY OVERCAME HER BUS ANXIETY

## The Special Skills That Helped Lily Feel Better:

- **Grounding-** When Lily felt nervous, she looked out the window and noticed all the details around her: colorful houses, trees, animals, and people. Focusing on what she could see helped calm her butterfly feelings.

- **Seeking Support-** Lily talked to her new friend Milo on the bus. Sharing her feelings and making a friend helped her feel less alone and more comfortable.

- **Accepting Help-** Lily let her mom give her advice about looking out the window. Sometimes letting others help us makes everything easier!

- **Remember:** It's okay to feel nervous about new things. When you use these special skills like Lily did, you might discover that your new adventure is even more wonderful than you imagined!

# IT'S FUN TO RIDE THE BUS!

## About DATTCO, Inc.

DATTCO is a premier transportation company headquartered in Southern New England since 1924. With over one hundred years of industry experience, DATTCO has been providing high-quality transportation solutions, including a motorcoach division for charters, shuttles, and tour services, a school bus division, and more. For additional information, please get in touch with *Marketing@DATTCO.com* or visit our website at *DATTCO.com*.

— **DATTCO**